Dear Parent:
Your child's love of reading starts here!

Every child learns to read in a different way and at his or her own speed. Some go back and forth between reading levels and read favorite books again and again. Others read through each level in order. You can help your young reader improve and become more confident by encouraging his or her own interests and abilities. From books your child reads with you to the first books he or she reads alone, there are I Can Read Books for every stage of reading:

SHARED READING
Basic language, word repetition, and whimsical illustrations, ideal for sharing with your emergent reader

BEGINNING READING
Short sentences, familiar words, and simple concepts for children eager to read on their own

READING WITH HELP
Engaging stories, longer sentences, and language play for developing readers

READING ALONE
Complex plots, challenging vocabulary, and high-interest topics for the independent reader

ADVANCED READING
Short paragraphs, chapters, and exciting themes for the perfect bridge to chapter books

I Can Read Books have introduced children to the joy of reading since 1957. Featuring award-winning authors and illustrators and a fabulous cast of beloved characters, I Can Read Books set the standard for beginning readers.

A lifetime of discovery begins with the magical words "I Can Read!"

Visit www.icanread.com for information
on enriching your child's reading experience.

I Can Read Book® is a trademark of HarperCollins Publishers.

Epic: M.K. Saves the Day
Epic © 2013 Twentieth Century Fox Film Corporation. All Rights Reserved. Manufactured in China. No part of this book may be used or reproduced in any manner whatsoever without written permission except in the case of brief quotations embodied in critical articles and reviews. For information address HarperCollins Children's Books, a division of HarperCollins Publishers, 195 Broadway, New York, NY 10007.
www.icanread.com
Library of Congress catalog card number: 2012953622
ISBN 978-0-06-220991-7

Typography by Rick Farley

17 SCP 10 9 8 7 6 5 4 3 ❖ First Edition

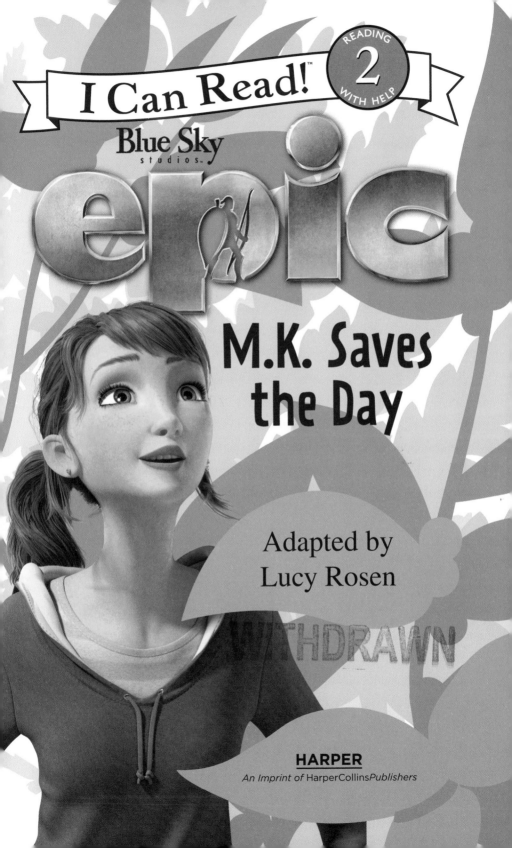

Blue Sky
STUDIOS™

epic

M.K. Saves the Day

Adapted by
Lucy Rosen

HARPER
An Imprint of HarperCollinsPublishers

Meet Mary Katherine.

(That's M.K. for short.)

She lives with her father,

Professor Bomba.

Professor Bomba is on a quest.

All day long

he scans the forest

for tiny creatures

he believes live there.

He's even set up

special cameras to prove they exist.

M.K. thinks her dad
is a pretty weird guy,
who doesn't live
in the real world.

"Tiny forest people aren't real, Dad. You've never even seen one!"

"Just because you don't see something, doesn't mean it's not there," he says.

M.K. doesn't listen.

She is tired of her dad's quest.

She thinks it is foolish.

One day, M.K. decides
to leave her dad's house
and go off on her own.
But her dad's dog, Ozzy,
dashes toward the forest.
M.K. chases after Ozzy,
going deeper and deeper
into the woods
until she is lost.

Something glowing floats by—
a tiny pod—and M.K. catches it.
Suddenly, M.K. shrinks down until
she is teeny tiny!
Now M.K. is on the forest floor
surrounded by other tiny people.

"You're real!" She gasps.

M.K. can't believe

her dad was right!

"Of course we're real!
We're the Jinn. And I'm Ronin,"
said a serious warrior.
"I'm the leader of the Leafmen.
We are protectors of the forest."

A young Leafman swoops over.

He joins M.K. and Ronin.

"Hey, I'm Nod. What's up?"

He smirks.

"What's going on?" asks M.K.

Ronin explains how

Queen Tara chose a pod to bloom.

"It is the key to the life of this forest."

Ronin continues,

"We must take the pod to Nim Galuu.

He will know how to make it bloom.

Come on, we'll travel by bird."

"You're with me, M.K.!" Nod grins.

17

"Can you slow down?" M.K. asks Nod.

"No time—the Boggans

want to steal the pod from us

so the forest will rot away."

As they fly, M.K. sees what the
Boggans have destroyed.
"Don't worry—you're safe with me!"

"Who are the Boggans?" M.K. asks.

Suddenly, M.K. turns and sees a group

of ugly, mean, buglike creatures

coming after them.

"Those are the Boggans!" Nod cries.

M.K. and Nod are chased
by a Boggan on a grackle.
They try to outfly him,
but suddenly there are
Boggans everywhere!

M.K. and Nod decide
they can escape better on foot.
They start to run, and then Nod
pulls M.K. out of the path
of an arrow.
They tumble into a pit.

M.K. turns and sees a mouse.

She doesn't think it can be fiercer

than the Boggans.

But Nod pulls her away.

M.K. knows they need more help.

She goes to find her dad.

When she gets home,

Ozzy is excited to see her.

M.K. keeps looking for her dad.

He has spent his whole life

searching for the Jinn.

She can't let the Boggans

destroy them!

M.K. decides the best way
to get her father's attention
is by using his own system.
She and Nod look for one
of his cameras.

"Dad! Dad!" M.K. calls
into one of Bomba's cameras.
Bomba is surprised to see her.
"My word! How did you get
so small?" he cries.
"No time to explain," says M.K.
"Hurry, Dad!"

Bomba races into the forest to help
the Jinn defeat the Boggans.
The pod blooms in the moonlight,
and the forest is restored
to its beautiful state.

M.K. shoots back to her

normal size.

Bomba is happy to see

his daughter again.

M.K. hugs her dad tightly.

When they get home,

M.K. and Bomba study the Jinn

together.

M.K. decides her dad is not

so strange after all.

"I thought I lost you," he says.

Because of his inventions,

the two of them can

watch over her new friends.

But best of all,

they can be together

and believe in each other.

31901062932977